Title: Squirrel Me Timbers
R.L.: 2.6
PTS: 0.5
TST: 179781

SQUIRREL me Timbers

by
LOUISE PIGOTT

Picture Window Books
a capstone imprint

Deep in the forest
and high in the trees,
lived a squirrel named Sammy
who dreamed of the seas.

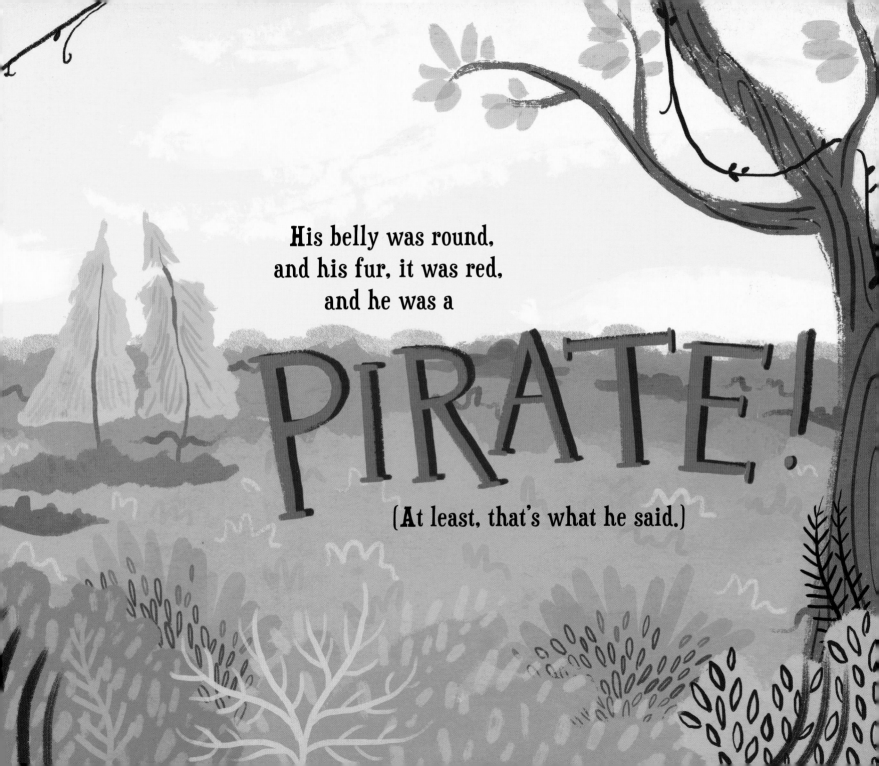

His belly was round,
and his fur, it was red,
and he was a

PIRATE!

(At least, that's what he said.)

"AHOY, MATEYS!"

cried Sammy,
light on his toes.

"Today's an adventure —
have you had one of those?

Come now, me hearties,
we'll have us some fun!

You'd better keep up
with me as I run!"

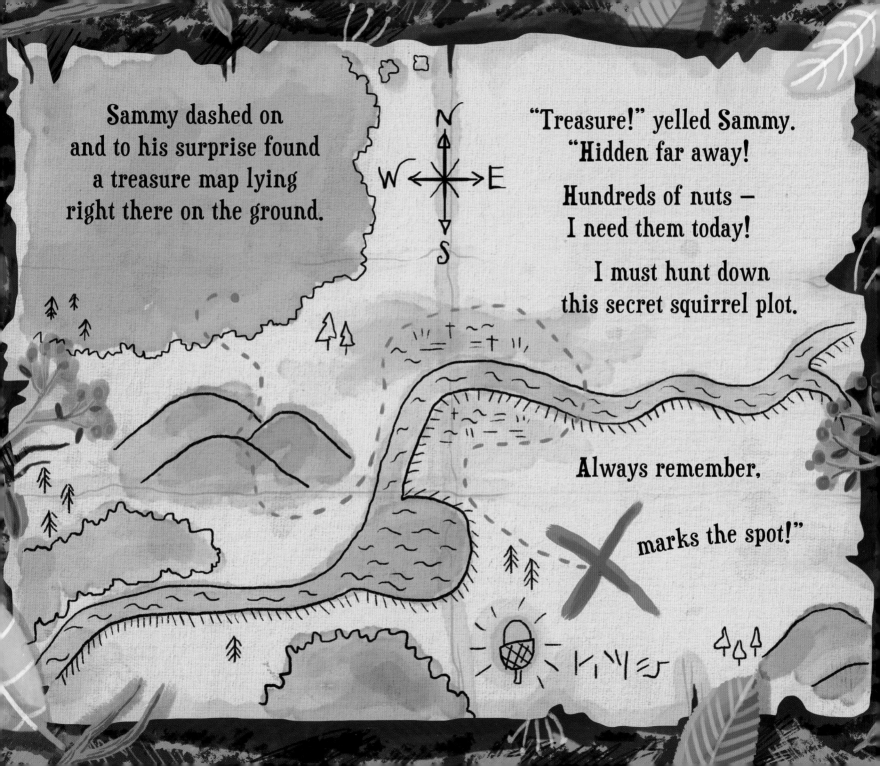

Sammy dashed on
and to his surprise found
a treasure map lying
right there on the ground.

"Treasure!" yelled Sammy.
"Hidden far away!

Hundreds of nuts —
I need them today!

I must hunt down
this secret squirrel plot.

Always remember,

marks the spot!"

Sammy was daring
and full of great skill,
so like a ball from a cannon
he shot down the hill!

But hidden by darkness were
thick spiky thistles . . .

"YOWCH!"

Sammy shouted.
"My bum's full of bristles!"

Pick out those prickles —
a hedgehog you're not!

We still have to find
where X marks the spot.

Now deep in the dark,
there lurked something scary . . .

SWISH! SNAP!
SPLASH!

Sammy, be wary!

Something in the water began to stir . . .
it gave Sammy goose bumps under his fur.

Shiny teeth fixed in a frightening smile,
this lake was home to . . .

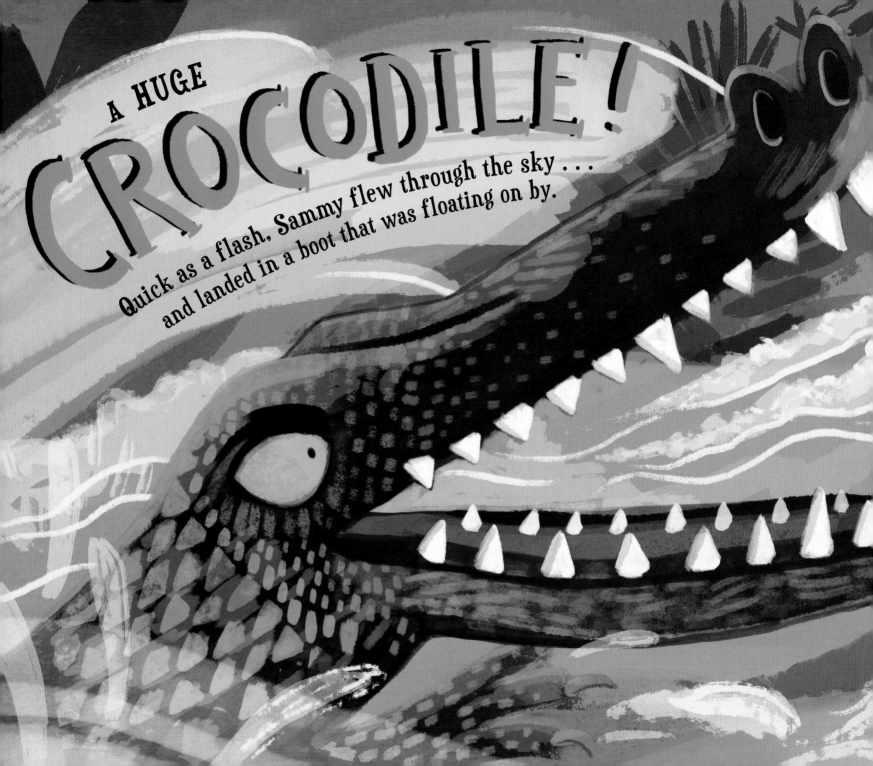

A HUGE CROCODILE!

Quick as a flash, Sammy flew through the sky . . .
and landed in a boot that was floating on by.

"'Tis a vessel!" he said.
"Although it be smelly,
I'll sail me away from that
beast's hungry belly!"

Come on now, Sammy,
a croc's snack you're not!

We still have to find
where **X** marks the spot.

Sammy flew down the river.
He really got going!

His ship wasn't so stinky
when the breeze started blowing.

The marshes looked eerie,
and Sammy felt daunted.

It wasn't just the wind wailing,
the whole place was . . .

HAUNTED!

Run away, Sammy,
from this spooky trap!

We're nearly at X marks
the spot on the map!

"We've made it!" cried Sammy,
but his eyes grew wide.

"There's no treasure here!
Those mapmakers lied!"

HUMPH!

WHACK!

"Not one single nut,
no bounty for me."

And so, in a fit,
Sammy kicked a tree.

There was a rumble and grumble
as Sammy howled in pain.

"Great!" he cried crossly.
"Now here comes the rain!"

But this was a shower
like no other foretold . . .

THOUSANDS OF IT'S NUTS.

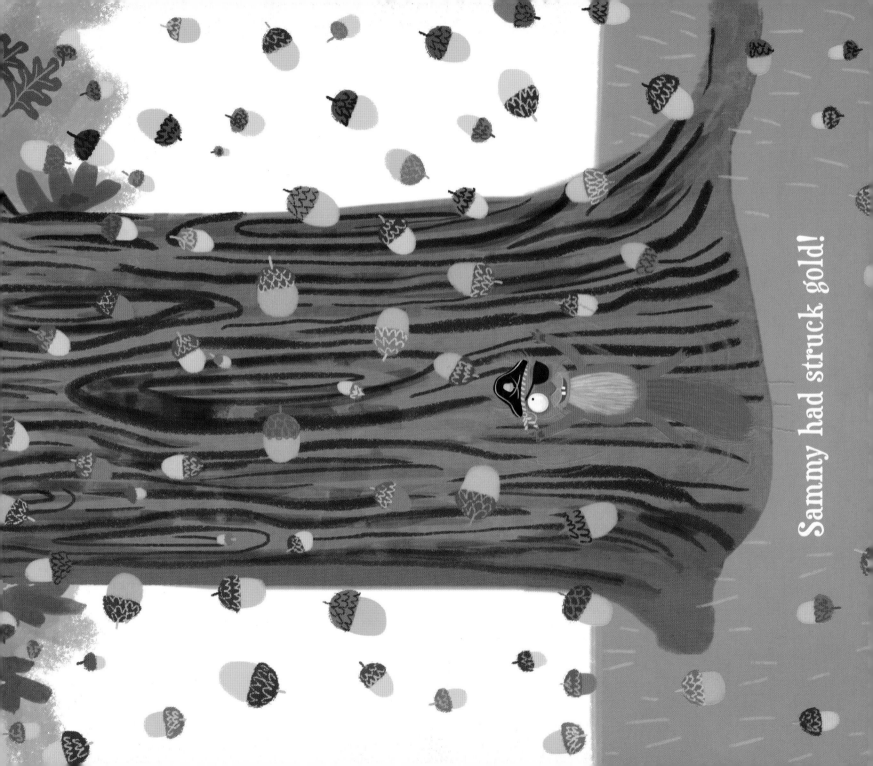

Sammy had struck gold!

Captain Hazelnut

You see, years ago, away from the seas,
some squirrels buried the treasure
they'd found from the trees.

Their treasure grew tall
and now hung overhead.

And they too were **PIRATES!**
(**At** least, that's what they said . . .)

About the Creator

Louise Pigott is an author and illustrator from Cambridge, United Kingdom. She received a First Class Bachelors of Arts Degree from De Montfort University, Leicester, in 2009. After graduating, Louise embarked upon a career as a freelance illustrator, working successfully within the greeting card and advertising industries, before pursuing her dream of writing and illustrating for children. *Squirrel Me Timbers* is Louise's first solo creation within children's publishing.

Squirrel Me Timbers is published by Picture Window Books,
a Capstone imprint
1710 Roe Crest Drive
North Mankato, Minnesota 56003
www.mycapstone.com

Text and illustrations © 2016 Louise Pigott

Library of Congress Cataloging-in-Publication Data
Pigott, Louise, author, illustrator.
 Squirrel me timbers / by Louise Pigott.
    pages cm

Summary: Sammy the squirrel dreams of being a pirate, so when he finds a treasure map, he sets out on an adventure to find the treasure.

ISBN 978-1-62370-652-4 (paper over board) -- ISBN 978-1-4795-9177-0 (library binding) -- ISBN 978-1-4795-9179-4 (ebook pdf)

1. Squirrels--Juvenile fiction. 2. Treasure troves--Juvenile fiction. 3. Pirates--Juvenile fiction. 4. Adventure stories. 5. Stories in rhyme. [1. Stories in rhyme. 2. Squirrels--Fiction. 3. Buried treasure--Fiction. 4. Pirates--Fiction. 5. Adventure and adventurers--Fiction.] I. Title.

PZ8.3.P558648Sq 2016

[E]--dc23

2015024329

Printed in China.
092015   009206S16